Rachel Elliot

illustrated by
Karen Sapp

Wide Awake Jake

PaRragon

Bath · New York · Singapore · Hong Kong · Cologne · Delhi · Melbourne

Jake couldn't sleep.
He lay on his back.
He lay on his tummy.

He even lay upside down.
But it was **no** good.

He was **still**
wide awake.

So Jake got up and went downstairs...

HUFF

PUFF

HUFFITY

PUFF

"I can't sleep," huffed Jake.

"Try counting sheep," said Dad.

But Jake didn't think **that** would help.

"Pretend you're a little bear,
going to sleep for the winter,"
said Mom.

Jake thought that **could** work.

So he went back upstairs...

pad

pad

pad

Jake curled up inside his blanket.

"I'm a little bear,

grrr, grrr,"

he growled.

But then he heard noises.

What if it was a great BIG bear?
It might have long, sharp claws
and huge, yellow teeth!

And his fur was very itchy.

Jake, the little bear,
was still wide awake.
So he got up

and went downstairs...

THUMP
BUMP
CLUMPITY
THUMP!

"I can't sleep," grumbled Jake.

"Count to a million," said Dad.

Jake didn't think **that** would help.

"Pretend you're a little mouse,
going to sleep in a mousehole,"
said Mom.

Jake thought that **could** work.

So he went back upstairs...

squeak

squeak

squeak

Jake crawled to the bottom of his bed.

But then he heard noises.

It might be a
big
fat
cat!!!

"Eek!" squeaked Jake,
the little mouse.

HURRY

FLURRY

SCURRY

"I can't sleep," worried Jake.
Dad just sighed.

Jake didn't think **that** was very helpful.

"Pretend you're a baby bird
in your nest,"
said Mom.

Jake thought it was worth a try.

So he went back upstairs...

flutter

flutter

flutter

Jake pulled his pillow under the covers.

"I'm a baby bird,
sitting in my nest,"
he whispered.

But his feathers kept

making him sneeze.

Then he
heard
noises!

Somebody was
pulling the
covers
down...

It was a big, hairy bear!

No, it didn't have any claws.

It was a fat, scary cat!

No, it didn't have a tail.

It was a big, scowly owl!

No, it didn't have a beak.

It was Mom!

Mom put the pillows straight.
She tucked Jake in,
nice and tight.

"You're my **brave** little Jake,
safe in your very own bed,"
said Mom.

"Now close your eyes.
It's time to sleep."

And with a growly yawn,

and a mouse-quiet wink,

and a fluttery blink,

Jake, the little boy,
was fast asleep.

For Mum and Robin
R.E.

For Grandad,
a special book for a special man
K.S.

Text © Rachel Elliot 2004
Illustrations © Karen Sapp 2004

This edition published by Parragon in 2007
Parragon
Queen Street House
4 Queen Street
Bath BA1 1HE, UK

Published by arrangement with
Meadowside Children's Books,
185 Fleet Street, London EC4A 2HS

ISBN 978-1-4054-9539-4
Printed in China